Baby Shower

Baby
Shower

JANE BRESKIN ZALBEN

WITHDRAWN

A NEAL PORTER BOOK
ROARING BROOK PRESS
NEW YORK

Zoe wanted a pet more than
anything in the whole world.

She thought about it when she woke up in the morning,

before she went to sleep,   and even when she dreamed.

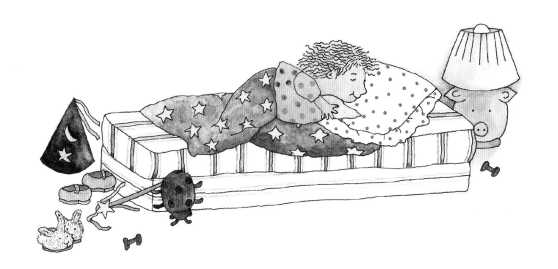

She'd stare at dogs on street corners,

cats curled up in windows,   and squirrels in the garden.

One day, while Mama was on the phone she overheard Zoe: "I'm petless in Port Washington!"

To take her mind off things, Mama suggested, "Why don't you help me with Aunt Ellie's baby shower?"

"What's a baby shower?" Zoe asked.

"A party before her baby's born."

"Will I get any presents?
Like maybe a pet?"

Mama sighed so loud you could hear her across town.

Zoe, hoping to get on her good side,
drew invitations and licked stamps
until her tongue tasted like sawdust.

Then she made a gift
and wrapped it with a bow.

That evening, when Papa tucked her in,
her mind was swirling with excitement.

I'm going to be a big cousin!

During the night, while Zoe was falling asleep, she heard the pitter-patter of rain on her windowsill.
The sky grew dark and strange.
Then there was a shower. A baby shower!
Of all kinds of babies:
ducklings, piglets,
cubs, kittens,
puppies,
and more.

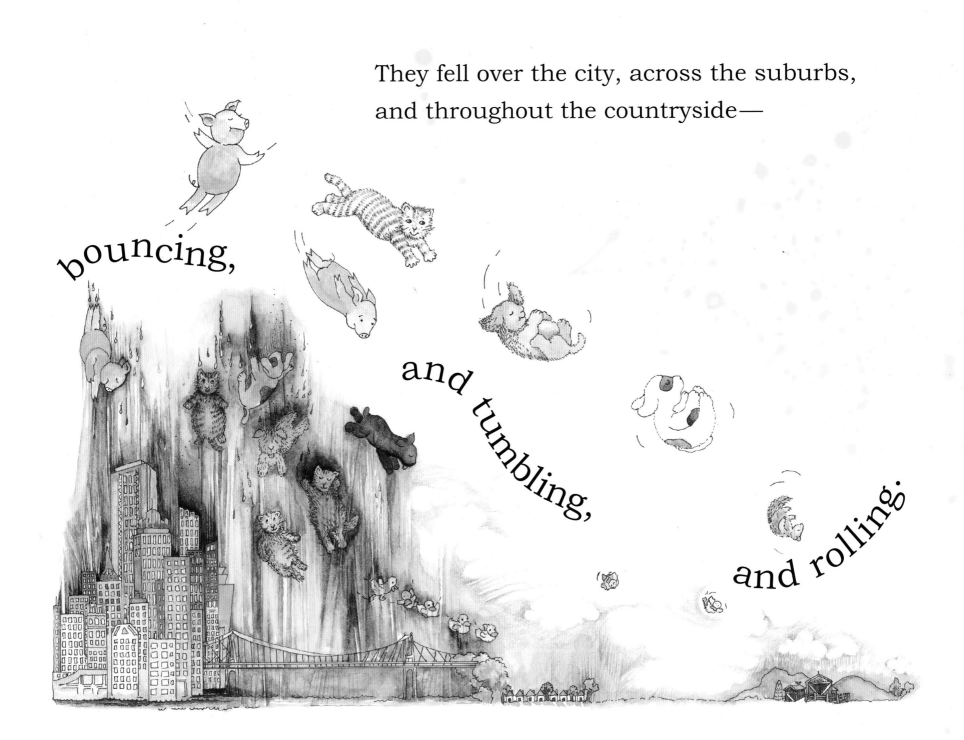

They fell over the city, across the suburbs, and throughout the countryside—

bouncing, and tumbling, and rolling.

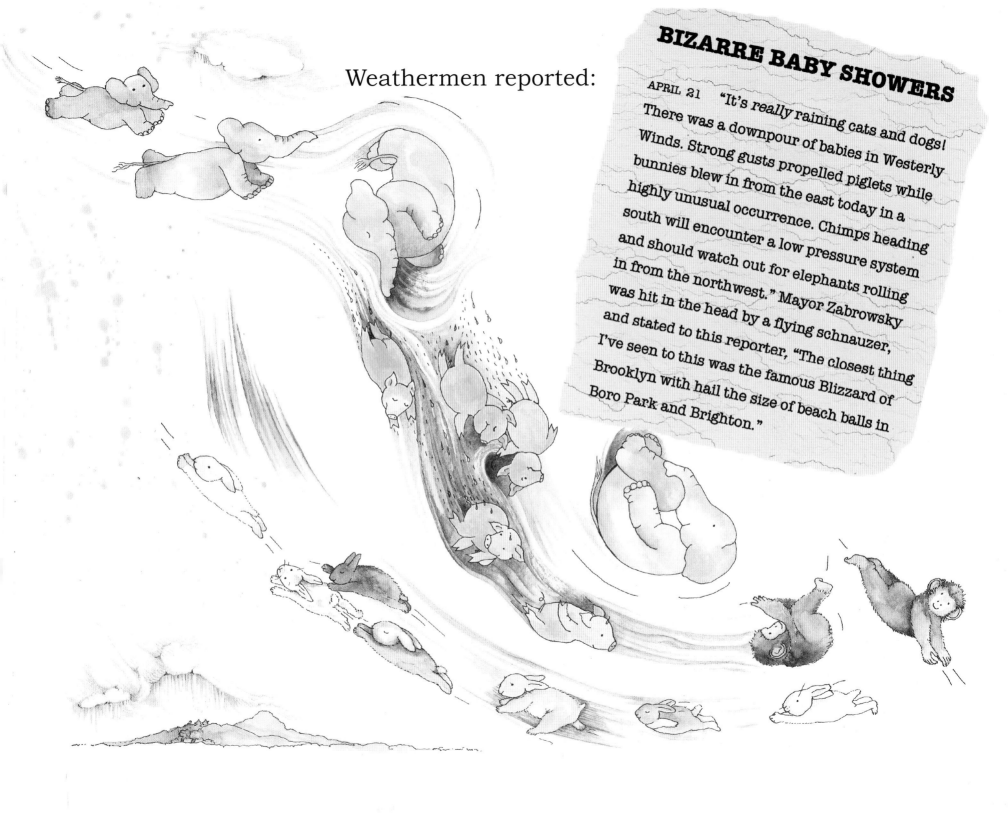

Weathermen reported:

BIZARRE BABY SHOWERS

APRIL 21 "It's really raining cats and dogs! There was a downpour of babies in Westerly Winds. Strong gusts propelled piglets while bunnies blew in from the east today in a highly unusual occurrence. Chimps heading south will encounter a low pressure system and should watch out for elephants rolling in from the northwest." Mayor Zabrowsky was hit in the head by a flying schnauzer, and stated to this reporter, "The closest thing I've seen to this was the famous Blizzard of Brooklyn with hail the size of beach balls in Boro Park and Brighton."

Rabbits rained on rooftops.

Turtles tangled traffic!

Lambs lolled on lawns.

Schools and offices closed,
museums and libraries, too.

Pet stores stayed open very late.

Babies were everywhere.

At parks,

beaches,

farms,

and zoos.

The day of the baby shower, Zoe put
on a new dress with matching socks,
honey-brown shoes, and two sparkly barrettes.

"Is it a boy or a girl?" one of the guests asked.

Aunt Ellie just smiled. "I hope so," she answered.

Zoe smiled, too, gazing up at the sky.

Aunt Ellie unwrapped Zoe's gift—a painting
she'd made of a cloud with animals pouring down.
Underneath she'd written, "baby shower."

"It's perfect!" said Aunt Ellie as
she hung it up on her refrigerator.
Mama beamed proudly.

As they were about to leave the party
lightning struck and thunder roared,
followed by a whimper,
a scratch, and a tiny bark.

On the steps in a puddle was
a puppy—warm and wet—
who smelled of
moist leaves.
Zoe's eyes widened.

"Can I keep him?" Zoe begged. "Ple-e-ze?"
The little puppy wagged his tail and looked up
with his big brown eyes. Mama nodded yes.
Zoe scooped the squiggly pup up in her arms.

She wrapped him in a towel, wiping away every last
raindrop until his fur was dry from head to tail.
"I'm going to name you Baby," she whispered.
Then the rain stopped, and the sun came out.

Weeks later, Aunt Ellie had twins—a boy and a girl!
When they came home from the hospital, Zoe brought
Baby over to visit. Zoe peeked at her newborn cousins.
"They look like the pictures of me when I was a baby!"

"See everyone, I have a new baby, too!"

Zoe smooched her puppy with a big sloppy kiss.

Baby gave Zoe the biggest and sloppiest kiss back!

And life couldn't get any better.

To our newest little addition,
and to babies everywhere—
human and otherwise.

A Neal Porter Book

Published by Roaring Brook Press

Roaring Brook Press is a division of Holtzbrinck Publishing Holdings Limited Partnership

175 Fifth Avenue, New York, New York 10010

www.roaringbrookpress.com

Distributed in Canada by H. B. Fenn and Company Ltd.

Cataloging-in-Publication Data is on file at the Library of Congress

ISBN: 978-1-59643-465-3

Roaring Brook Press books are available for special promotions and premiums.

For details contact: Director of Special Markets, Holtzbrinck Publishers.

First Edition April 2010

Book design by Jennifer Browne

Printed in April 2010 in China by Macmillan Production (Asia) Ltd., Kwun Tong, Kowloon, Hong Kong (Supplier Code: 10)

1   3   5   7   9   8   6   4   2